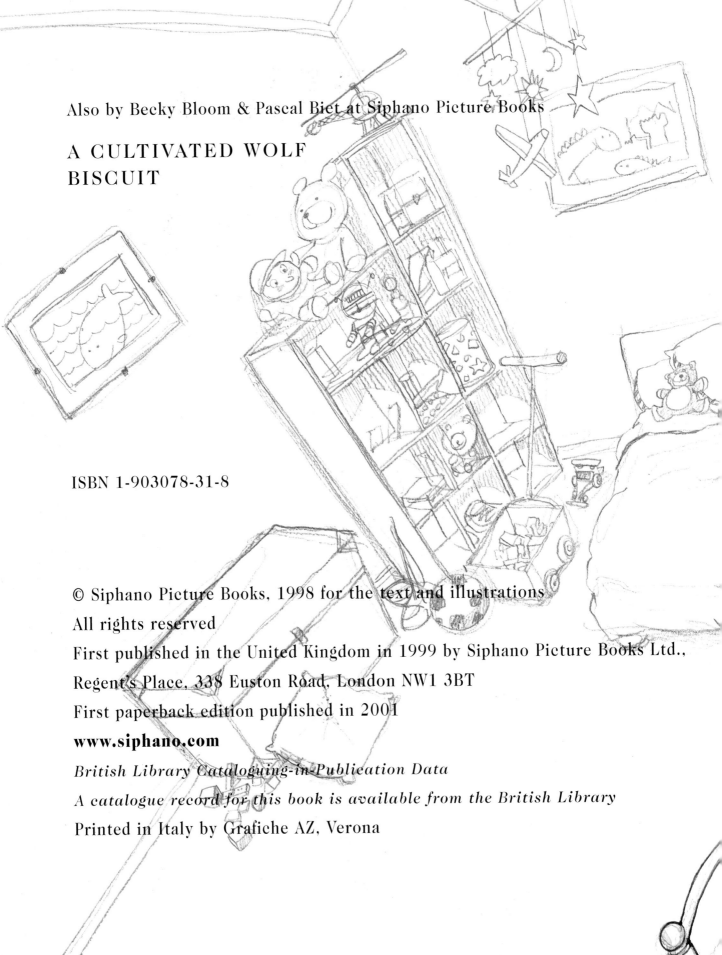

Also by Becky Bloom & Pascal Biet at Siphano Picture Books

A CULTIVATED WOLF
BISCUIT

ISBN 1-903078-31-8

© Siphano Picture Books, 1998 for the text and illustrations
First published in the United Kingdom in 1999 by Siphano Picture Books Ltd.,
Regent's Place, 338 Euston Road, London NW1 3BT
First paperback edition published in 2001
www.siphano.com

British Library Cataloguing-in-Publication Data
A catalogue record for this book is available from the British Library
Printed in Italy by Grafiche AZ, Verona

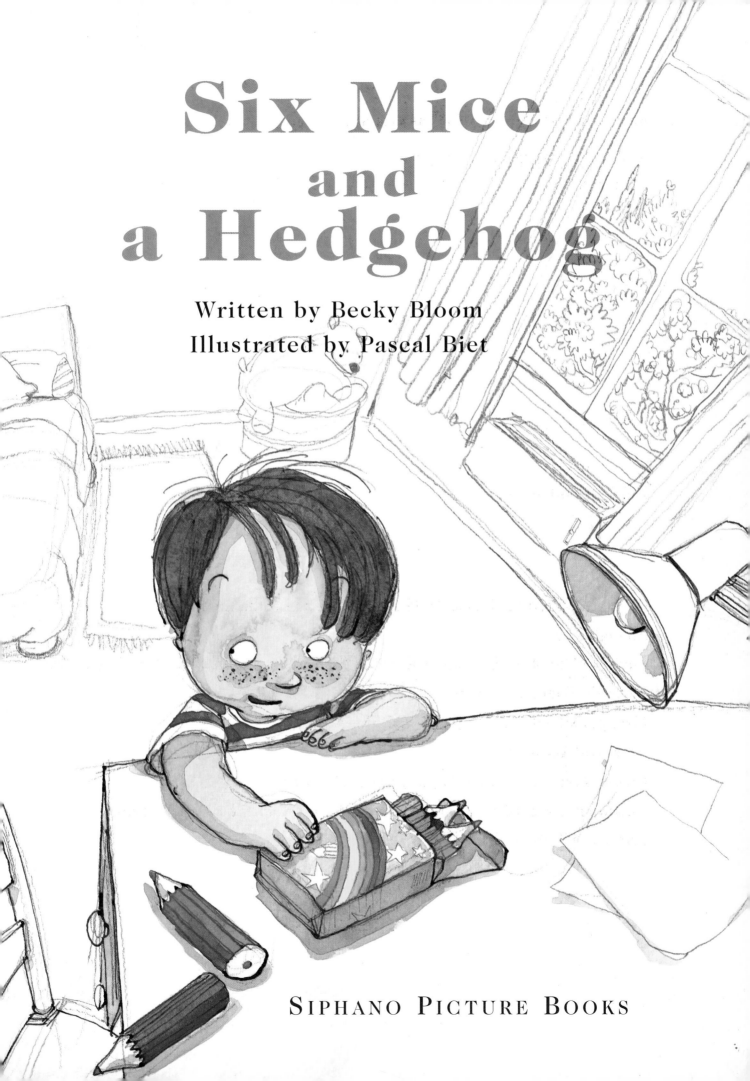

Six Mice
and
a Hedgehog

Written by Becky Bloom
Illustrated by Pascal Biet

SIPHANO PICTURE BOOKS

One day Reginald secretly borrowed his sister's box of colour pencils. She had said the pencils were magic, and he wanted to see for himself.

"WARNING: Do not draw dangerous or mischievous animals" was printed on the cover of the box. But Reginald couldn't read yet. He closed the shutters of his room and began to draw on the bare wall. He drew a tiny car and coloured it red...

...and before he had
time to draw anything else
the car popped off the wall
and zoomed across the room.
Reginald would have loved to ride
on it but the car was way too tiny for
him. Who would be small enough to get
in this car? he wondered.

A mouse!

That was it! Reginald quickly sketched a mouse hole on the wall and drew a mouse above it. But the mouse didn't look quite right, and Reginald had to wipe it away and draw another...

...which wasn't right either; nor was
the next one, nor the one after that,
and so on, until six mice had been wiped
away. Reginald finally settled for
a hedgehog. It was much easier
to draw.

But as the hedgehog walked off the wall to explore Reginald's room, the six not-quite-right mice followed right behind. Each one of them had the very problem which made Reginald wipe it away in the first place, but none of them seemed to mind at all.

One had too big an ear, another too long a tail,
another too round a head. There were red noses,
crooked whiskers, long legs, fleecy fur. What
an extraordinary assortment of mice they were!

Reginald was delighted to have
company but his playmates were not
very civilised. They started fighting and soon spoiled
all the games. Only the hedgehog knew how to behave.

He had found the colour
pencils and was drawing
a glass of soda.

Then he sat on a comfortable pillow and began to read. And that is when the trouble began. Now that the mice had found out about the magic pencils, they started drawing all sorts of toys, all of them entirely inappropriate for indoors. And they jumped and hopped and raced around the room *shrieking* and *cheering.*

When there was no more room left to play because of
all the toys, they grabbed the colour pencils and
started drawing again. Earthworms
and butterflies and bees and bugs
of all sorts (the mice knew *not*
to draw any dangerous
animals) jumped off
the wall and crawled and
flew about the room.

What a mess they were making! Even the hedgehog contributed: his prickles had torn the pillow to pieces. Finally Reginald had an idea. He took the box of colour pencils away from the mice,

and, as fast as he could, he drew a teacher...

She was a very serious and respectable mouse-lady, with rimmed glasses and a book in her hand. And she looked just right!

"QUIET PLEASE!" she said firmly as she walked off the wall, and at once the mice were silent and a little embarrassed. "Come to me all of you," she instructed, taking the youngest mouse by the hand. She was about to take them all back into the mouse hole and keep them busy there with nursery rhymes and games.

But then she looked around
Reginald's room, and thought it
most impolite to leave him
with such a mess. Taking
the colour pencils, she quickly
drew a broom, some soap, pails
of warm water, brushes and mops.

Then she had the mice and the hedgehog scrub all the pencil marks from the walls and the floor and the furniture, and put Reginald's room back in order.

And when all the toys were put away, the teacher drew a small cardboard box to hold all the little animals crawling and flying about the room; she planned to show them to her kindergarten mice.

Then the six mice apologised to Reginald and went quietly into the mouse hole. They dragged along the hedgehog who was quite reluctant to leave Reginald's room.

After the teacher and the animals left,
there were no signs of what had happened,
except for the tiny mouse hole which no one
had remembered to wipe away.

And sometimes, as Reginald lies in his bed
at night, if he listens carefully, he can still
hear chuckling and giggling coming out
of the wall.

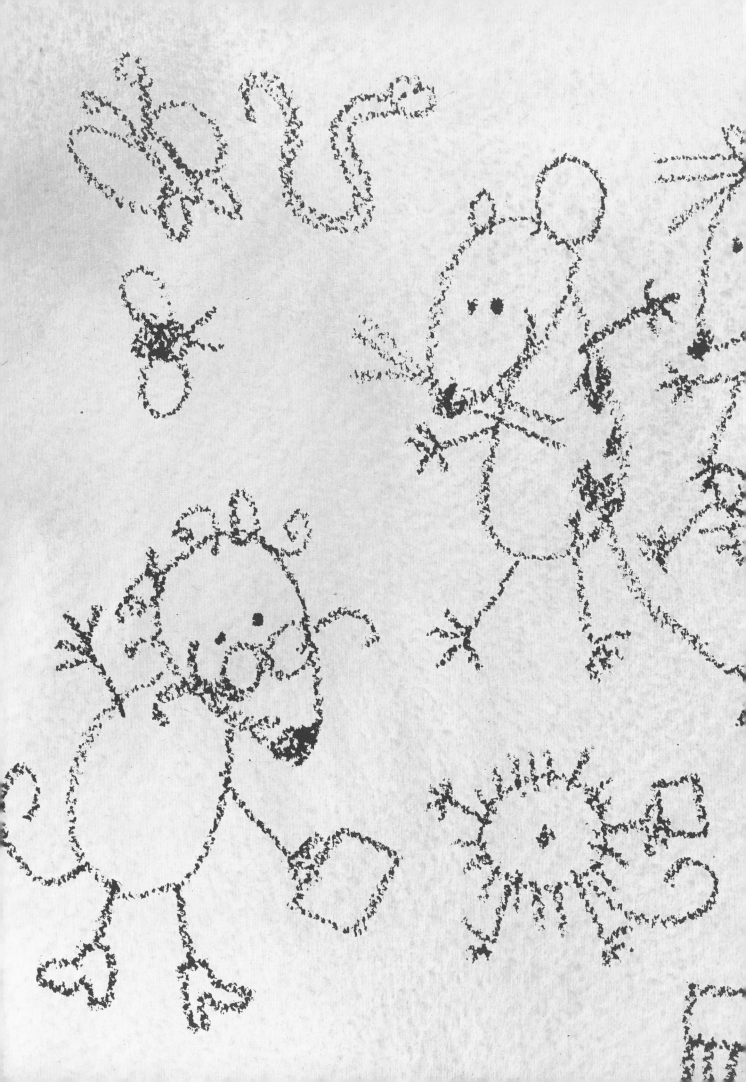

THREE WISHES, MASTER DOG
by Gianluca Garofalo

"Among the many strangely unsatisfying re-tellings of traditional tales on the market at the moment, it is wonderful to find a book like this that draws on some knowledge of the canon, but makes no excuses for its fable-like simplicity... ...a lively book that offers a sure-fire starting point for a classroom discussion."

Siân Hughes in Child Education

LOST: ONE DOG, GREEN
by Pascal Biet

"...well written and the illustrations are wacky enough to please the 4s – 6s"
Financial Times

"...an engaging story with some unexpected surprises and a lively humorous tone."
Angela Redfern in The School Librarian

A CULTIVATED WOLF
by Becky Bloom and Pascal Biet

"[A] delightful, witty picture book...."
Lyndsey Fraser in The Guardian (Children's Book of the Week)

"Tributes to the civilising influence of story, books and reading are rarely as engaging as they are here!"
Robert Dunbar in The School Librarian

"It's a story with a moral – but a very palatable one. And the pictures are great."
Kit Spring in The Observer

A PIG IS MOVING IN!
by Claudia Fries

"The illustrations are a delight..."
Wendy Cooling, Literacy & Learning

"Lovely water-colour illustrations and lively, humorous text make this an attractive book..."
Sybil Hannavy in The School Librarian

"A moral fable de nos jours, rescued from goody-goody PC-ness by sturdy illustration. Useful first read-alone."
Financial Times